W9-ADO-403

Monster Boy and the Snow Day

BY CARL EMERSON
ILLUSTRATED BY LON LEVIN

visit us at www.abdopublishing.com

Published by Magic Wagon, a division of the ABDO Group, 8000 West 78th Street, Edina, Minnesota 55439.
Copyright © 2011 by Abdo Consulting Group, Inc. International copyrights reserved in all countries. All rights reserved. No part of this book may be reproduced in any form without written permission from the publisher.

Looking Glass Library™ is a trademark and logo of Magic Wagon.

Printed in the United States of America, North Mankato, Minnesota.
052010
092010

 THIS BOOK CONTAINS AT LEAST 10% RECYCLED MATERIALS.

Text by Carl Emerson
Illustrations by Lon Levin
Edited by Nadia Higgins
Interior layout and design by Emily Love
Cover design by Emily Love

Library of Congress Cataloging-in-Publication Data

Emerson, Carl.
  Monster Boy and the snow day / by Carl Emerson ; illustrated by Lon Levin.
    p. cm. — (Monster Boy)
  ISBN 978-1-60270-779-5
  [1. Monsters—Fiction. 2. Snow—Fiction.] I. Levin, Lon, ill. II. Title.
  PZ7.E582Mnw 2010
  [E]—dc22
                    2010007077

Marty Onster felt a knot in his gut as soon as he woke up.
It was Monday—time to head back to school.

Normally, that wouldn't bother Marty. But today he was supposed to present his book report to the class. His choice, *Hairy Monster and the Deadly Shallows*, was really long. He still hadn't finished it.

Marty stumbled down the stairs and saw his parents staring out the window. They were standing in a puddle of drool.

That's when Marty realized he couldn't even see out the window. It was snowing like crazy!

"Snow day?" Marty yelled. "Is it a snow day?"

"It sure is!" Marty's dad said. "Look how deep the animals' tracks are! They'll lead us right to breakfast!"

"I'll get ketchup!" Marty's mom announced.

"But Mom, Dad," Marty said, "please . . . don't eat *all* the squirrels again. I like some of them."

It was too late. They were already out the door.

Marty sighed. More than anything he wanted to be a normal kid. How was he supposed to pass as a human with parents like that?

Marty knew what would cheer him up.
He quickly dialed his best friend, Sally
Weet. "Let's go sledding!" Marty cried.
"The hill will be really slick today!"

Soon, Marty and Sally were speeding
down Breakneck Hill. They had it all to
themselves.

Just when they were starting to get tired, Bart Ully showed up with a couple of his friends.

The guys started digging at the bottom of the hill.

"What do you think you're doing?" Marty challenged.

"What's it to you, Fangtooth?" Bart shot back. "We're building a jump."

Marty didn't like the look in Bart's eyes.

"It will be the biggest jump ever," Bart continued. "It's going to be an awesome ride—*if* you have the guts to try it."

Marty felt the hairs on his back start to poke through his jacket. Bart was getting him mad again, and Marty just couldn't help it. He was turning into a monster.

"What's the matter, Marty?" Bart said. "You're not going to turn blue on me again, are you?"

"Look, why don't you make your jump just a little smaller and move it to the side?" Sally said. "Then people who don't want to go off it won't have to."

"And you won't wreck the hill for everyone," Marty added as he and Sally started to climb the hill.

But Bart and his friends didn't stop. Soon the jump stretched across the bottom of the hill.

After they finished making their jump, Bart and his
friends climbed up to Sally and Marty.

"I don't want to go off that jump," Sally said.

But Bart's friends weren't worried.
They hopped on their sleds
and sped off.

"So, what's it going to be, Onster?" Bart said. "You're always flying around all crazy. Are you scared of a little jump?"

"Not scared, just smart," Marty said.

"Well, maybe Sally will go then!" Bart said. Sitting on his sled, he rammed into the back of Sally's legs. Before Marty could do anything, they took off down the hill.

Marty's eyes burned. Fur shot out the top of his jacket. Claws poked through his mittens and boots.

In a flash, he was at the jump. Marty was a blue-and-white blur as he worked to save his friend.

Sally and Bart sped down to the bottom, but they didn't fly off the jump. They went up, up the side of the giant wall that Marty had created in its place. At the top, Sally calmly stepped off the sled.

Sally looked at Marty and smiled. Then, she gave the sled a little bump. It sped down the other side of the wall.

"Nice job, Marty!" Sally said.

"Thanks," Marty replied, "but I don't think Bart likes his jump so much anymore."

Contain Your Inner Monster
Tips from Marty Onster

 If a situation feels dangerous, trust your gut.
Don't be scared. Be smart.

 It's great to stick up for your friends. But unless you have
monster powers, get help from a grown-up if a friend
is in danger.

 Next time you feel like exploding into a monster,
take a deep breath. Count to ten.
Then decide what to do.